About the author

Heather Buckley is a twenty-eight-year-old woman living in the Southwestern region of the United States. Heather is a writer, teacher, student of Yoga, lightworker and an artist. She is passionate about supporting women and uplifting the global collective energy of the world through education, empowerment and expression.

Heather was inspired to write *Wildflower* based upon her own adventures living and working in San Diego, California. She is passionate about mentoring young women and providing them with a new paradigm of relationships and success.

With a little help from her loved ones, Heather is surviving her own winding road and the potholes that inevitably surface as she moves throughout her life.

WILDFLOWER

HEATHER BUCKLEY

WILDFLOWER

Vanguard Press

VANGUARD PAPERBACK

A CIP catalogue record for this title is
available from the British Library.

ISBN 978 1 80016 410 9

*Vanguard Press is an imprint of
Pegasus Elliot MacKenzie Publishers Ltd.*
www.pegasuspublishers.com

First Published in 2022

**Vanguard Press
Sheraton House Castle Park
Cambridge England**

Printed & Bound in Great Britain

Dedication

This book is dedicated to all of the bright, young women who have the ability to change the trajectory of this world.

Acknowledgements

This book is for anyone who has ever doubted themselves, their infinite beauty and their undeniable worth. It is for anyone that has experienced trauma, grief, anxiety, depression, struggle or loss of hope. I want you to know that there is a brighter tomorrow. That your struggles have purpose. Your pain has a purpose. You are being shown the dark so that you can move past it into the light. Back into your internal glow.

I would like to thank my family, without whose love and support I would not be here. To my mother, who raised me and gave me everything, thank you. To my father, who is no longer here, Godspeed and stay in touch. To my sister, who is the voice of reason for so many of my troubled days, I owe you. To my brother, whose practical intellect has moved me forward in many ways, I am grateful.

To my best friends, I could not survive this roller coaster ride called life without you. To my friends near and far, there is no greater gift than to know you. To all of those in New Mexico, thank you for shaping my journey and showing me the world.

To the people of my past, I see you. Honour you. Understand you. To those who have hurt me and to those I have hurt, I acknowledge the greater web we have weaved together. And finally, to the journey itself, there is no sweeter feeling than you, a life that is incredibly, irrevocably and inexplicably mine and mine alone.

Words from the Author

Wildflower is a novella inspired by the events that have taken place in the first twenty-eight years of my life. Yet this book is so much more than simply the culmination of my life alone. It is a tall tale inspired by the incredible human beings that I have met on my journey both near and far, some good, some bad, some light, some dark. It is a coming-of-age story that will tug at the heartstrings of most and open the eyes of those yet to ever take part on such a journey.

Wildflower is a beacon of hope for women everywhere. It shows us the magical things that can happen when a young woman chooses herself over everything else. Kate mirrors to us the struggles within humanity of the modern woman. She aims to navigate the world with kindness and grace. She shows up for her family and friends with unwavering love. She dominates her career and climbs up the business ladder without fail. Most of all, she stays open to love in her heart.

This novella was written for anyone who has even taken the harder choice in life and didn't know where it would lead them. *Wildflower* is a story for the modern millennial. It puts to rest co-dependent love stories of the past and carves a path for a new kind of romance. It highlights the power of a woman who falls in love with life itself and shows the world that she is unstoppable in that unwavering belief.

I hope that you, the reader, enjoy the everyday fumbles of this beautiful yet messy young girl. I hope that you experience the magic that she feels in everyday moments. I hope that you feel the romanticism of embarking on the journey of your dreams, even if you have no clue where it will end up.

I hope that you laugh, you cry and mostly, I hope that you feel. I hope that you feel your heart expand and contract as you read through the pages of this book simply because you are feeling what it means to experience being human… So, here's to the eternal quest of the heart we set out on… Once upon a time… cheers to you, dear reader.

With love, light and romance,
Heather

Chapter 1
Rags and Riches

The shrill buzz of the alarm clock pierced through the dim morning light. Kate rolled over groggily, half-shocked and half- annoyed as she checked out the clock. 5.55 a.m. She clicked the alarm off a little too forcibly, rolled out of bed and rolled her eyes along with it as she woke and stumbled across the dark room.

Kate entered her bathroom and flicked on the light. She glanced in the mirror under the bold fluorescent lighting and turned her head to the side gingerly. She touched a delicate finger to her cheekbone. There they were. Circles. The dull glisten of a shadow traced the area just underneath both of her eyes.

Kate was twenty-two. Yet in that moment, she felt inexplicably wise. All-knowing. Annoyed. Getting older was a piece of shit. Kate splashed her face with cold water, patted a pink towel against her cheeks and looked again into the mirror. Her face looked different somehow. It was a thought that had been hiding in the back of her mind for the past few months and only now was she faced with the ugly truth: she was aging.

Kate slid a thin arm into a black-and-white collared shirt. She squirmed under the itchy fabric as she buttoned it up and grimaced. Kate hated being buttoned up. She layered on her quintessential rose lip colour, a touch of dark mascara and tugged a strand of dark blonde wavy hair behind her right ear.

"Shit! I'm late," Kate yelped to herself. She grabbed her already-crammed bag, shoved her lipstick and phone into it with a vengeance and shivered as she ran to her car. She started her ancient CRV as she slowly backed into the road and noticed a touch of orange now joining the dark horizon. As she admired the beauty of the sunrise, her coffee cup tilted and spilled half of its contents onto her lap.

Off to a great start, she thought.

Kate slid behind the counter of the Harvest Cafe as she caught the time and winced. 7.02 a.m. Two minutes late. She tied her apron behind her back and gave an awkward yet apologetic grin to her manager, Dave. He was tall, gay, gorgeous and one of the very few people she could stand in this place.

A slender, doe-eyed blonde walked (somewhat glided) up to the register. Her black dress was tailored perfectly to fit the shape of her 5'9" hourglass figure. She was one of those women that oozed confidence and stature without ever opening their lips. She looked as if she owned the world. Probably because she had never before experienced a world that she did not, in fact, own.

Kate touched the turquoise gemstone against her throat. She never left her house without it.

"Almond milk matcha. No sugar." The doe-eyed blonde glanced at her phone as she pulled out a credit card thicker and heavier than the door of Kate's car.

"That'll be $5.50." Kate smiled, wondering if the woman could tell that she was secretly rolling her eyes on the inside.

The blonde walked away without hardly a glance and pranced over to a marbled table while she continued to look at her phone. She was unaffected by Kate. No tip. Kate was annoyed but not at all surprised. The people here held onto their money and they wanted everyone to know it.

A beautiful man walked through the French cafe doors. Kate's jaw dropped as she studied his chiselled jawbone, rugged locks and neatly fit blazer over what she could only be sure were washboard abs. Kate watched the man slide easily into the booth next to the doe-eyed blonde and give her a kiss on the cheek. The blonde hardly faltered as she photographed her matcha latte and typed up a quirky caption.

"I heard he owns half of the city." Dan smirked at Kate as he touched his hip next to hers.

They rested their heads into the crook of their palms as they ogled the beautiful couple together. "Make me a shot." Kate softly jabbed her elbow into Dan.

He laughed as he began to pat the espresso down to the perfect degree that he always did. Kate observed Dan's beautiful forearms and felt a glimmer of awe. Amidst the grumble of the coffee grinder, Kate felt her mind wander back to a somewhat less glamorous landscape.

An old blue pickup truck rolled down the winding hills of the New Mexican backcountry. Sunlight warmed the skin on Kate's face as a contented bubble of laughter escaped from her lips. The blue sky was lined with the kind of puffy white clouds that could only mean one thing: summer. Her palm grazed the wind outside of the pickup truck window and she glanced over at Cal. A baseball cap lay snug at his brow line and his dark skin gripped the wheel securely. The desert landscape was filled with cacti and dirt as they flew by and sped down the one-lane highway together. It was the kind of day that you knew that you would never forget, Kate thought, simply for the reason that it was inexplicably perfect in the most mundane of ways.

"Here, slacker." Dan pushed the pink cup toward Kate with a smirk.

"You're the best." She winked, and slugged down the bitter sweet liquid as she prepared to take on another day. *I really hate this place,* she thought to herself as she turned to the next customer.

Chapter 2
A Night Out

Eight hours later, Kate slugged through the door into her shared beach apartment, still smelling like the faint scent of coffee grounds and sweat. She kicked off her shoes, grabbed a bag of pita chips and collapsed into her bed. Her mind began to wander back to the doe-eyed blonde and her boyfriend's washboard abs when suddenly, her roommate, Zoe, popped in.

"Wanna go to the beach?" She grinned.

Zoe was full of life. She had grown up in Los Angeles and loved to party. Most people around here liked to party. Kate was the odd one out.

"Gimme five minutes." Kate smiled at Zoe and popped a pita chip into her rose-coloured mouth.

Thirty minutes later, the duo arrived at the ocean rocking bright bikinis and iced americanos. Zoe donned high-waisted jean shorts and two buns on the top of her head a la Baby Spice. Kate admired her beauty.

"I bet you anything that Joe won't wear a costume tonight." Zoe laughed.

Tonight, was Halloween. The biggest holiday of the year in the young beach town. *Exactly like the Movie* Mean Girls, *give or take the animal ears,* Kate thought.

Joe was Zoe's boyfriend. They were crazy for each other. They drove each other crazy too. They were always up and down. Fighting. Screaming. Making out. I was thrilled for her. I had heard a rumour from one of our guy friends last week that Joe was shopping for engagement rings.

Zoe deserved it. She grew up poor and was a first-generation American citizen. Her parents had worked hard to make it to Los Angeles. Zoe repaid her parents with a degree in marketing from UCLA and a weekend job at Sephora.

Kate and Zoe spent the remainder of the afternoon giggling at seagulls trying to steal their baby carrots and cooing at small babies on the hips of young mothers. The two had been waiting for what felt like eternity for Halloween to arrive. Kate begged Dan to give her the next morning off of work and he had obliged much easier than she had prepared for.

Kate rummaged through her closet and the many fabric choices she had popped out at her: sexy red satins and black lace, pink frothy dresses and white ribbed tees. Kate pulled out a black high-neck dress with cut-outs on the side. She added a shade darker of her usual rose lipstick and swept cream shimmer onto her eyelids. Zoe pranced in wearing silver booty shorts and a sequined bra, the line of her ass cheeks softly bulking out from under her shorts the way that all of the girls' butts around here did.

Zoe rolled her eyes at Kate. "Why do you look so grown up?" Kate had always gravitated towards a different era of style. "Well, you look pretty," she said. "Zach will be so into you."

Zach was Joe's buddy from college and your typical Southern California dipshit. Twenty-five, tall, with a huge penis and no manners to show for it.

"Maybe," Kate replied as she folded up a satin blouse and placed it back in the closet.

"Totally." Zoe walked away and dialled her boyfriend Joe up on the phone.

An hour later, the boys arrived. Kate checked herself out in the mirror and was pleased with her effort. Getting men to like her was one of the few things that came naturally to Kate. She knew exactly how to place her hand against her cheek and open her eyes wide, almost as if to signal to men, "Come rescue me."

Zach did seem to have his eye on her for his next serving of the female form. A few shots later, the group walked to the closest bar in the neighbourhood. Fog machines spewed out nauseous gas as drunken party girls teetered on their stilettos and clung onto their boat party chic fraternity boyfriends. Kate smiled at the bouncer as he checked her id. The squad entered the crowded bar and sauntered toward the servers.

"Want a drink?" Zach asked Kate.

"Vodka soda," Kate replied and parted her mauve lips.

Zoe was already showcasing her moves on the dance floor. Joe's hands grazed her hips as they grinded on each other and screamed out the words of whatever popular ballad blasted through the speakers. Kate grinned at her from the bar.

"What do you do for work?" Zach asked her dryly.

Kate glanced towards him. "Coffee shop," she replied and sipped the vodka soda. "But I teach yoga too. The barista gig is just to get me by."

Kate could see Zach's pupils dilate at the thought of her doing yoga and she could almost visualise the contorted acrobatic image that seemed to saturate his brain. It was annoying, she thought, how all men thought this way. But she was already getting drunk and Zoe was busy. Kate liked that she had this ability with men although it never seemed to get her anywhere past the weekend after. "What about you?" Kate said.

"Finance," Zach replied.

They nodded to each other and continued to sip their drinks.

Zach and Kate joined Zoe and Joe on the dance floor a few minutes later and she casually swayed her body as she ran her fingers through her hair.

"Come home with me," Zach whispered into Kate's hair.

"OK," she drunkenly murmured.

At two a.m., the bar closed. Kate grabbed Zoe's wrist. "I'm gonna go to his place," she whispered.

"OK, babe, just make sure you have condoms." Her soft eyes met Kate's and focused for a moment with concern before they passed back into a drunken haze. "Carry me, babe!" Zoe shouted to Joe. She hopped onto his back as they walked down the street happily together.

Zach grabbed Kate's hand but they didn't talk much. When she got to his place, it was cold, but clean. She glanced around to his nightstand at a baseball card collection and he kissed her, one hand already fumbling for her dress zipper. Three hours later, Kate lay awake staring at the ceiling wearing nothing but her lace black thong.

That morning, Zach rolled over lazily as Kate kissed him goodbye. She walked outside and blinked, surprised by the bright sunshine. She could smell the faint sea salt that always grazed the air in Southern California as she walked home. As Kate went to turn the lock to her front door, she heard a loud crunching noise. *BANG.* The door hit metal on metal as Kate's shoulder thrust into the door. Zoe had put the security lock on.

Kate walked around to the back alley, sighing as she sidestepped empty Coors Light cans and discarded Camel cigarettes boxes. She opened her window and removed the screen. Begrudgingly, she hoisted her torso onto the window as she jumped up. She could feel the metal edge of the window bottom carve into her midsection as she paused halfway. Kate squeezed her triceps and with one final thrust made it through the

window into her room. She glared as she shut the
window and collapsed onto her bed and slept through
the hazy afternoon.

Chapter 3
A Spiritual Awakening

Kate groggily awoke that evening with the faint scent of booze and cigarette smoke hanging slightly in her hair. She hated the queasy feeling of being hungover and went to shower off the sensation before her yoga teacher training. Kate loved yoga. She felt free every time she set foot in the studio and she imagined that Zoe felt something similar whenever she landed her feet onto the dance floor.

As Kate towelled off, she caught a glimmer of a bruise against her throat. A hickey. *FUCK.* This day was getting worse and worse. Kate combed her hair extra meticulously as she styled herself with a high bun and dark-rimmed glasses. She chose a cream scarf and wrapped it delicately around her neck. She looked into the mirror and was certain that everyone could smell the guilt and shame on her from a mile away.

Kate could have skipped the training that evening but the thought never crossed her mind once. Yoga gave her purpose and it came naturally to her. The feelings and words flowed naturally through her without trying whenever she was teaching yoga. It seemed to Kate as if she had lived a thousand lifetimes as a yoga teacher before and was simply allowing herself to wake up to the feeling of it in those sacred moments.

Kate took a cross-legged seat on the floor of the yoga studio and ran her hands over the soft hardwood floors beneath her. She took a deep inhale as if she could finally breathe for the first time in a very long time. Kate smiled at her friends as she pulled out a spiral notebook and pen to prepare for the lecture. Life seemed easier in yoga world, she thought to herself with a smile.

A radiant Indian woman stepped into the centre of the circle. She seemed to glow and glisten without any added makeup. The group joined hands as they always did at the beginning of lectures and took three breaths in union. The woman spoke of Chakras and Vedas and as the night went on, Kate felt a sleepy feeling overcome her.

Kate doodled a small flower on the upper right corner of her notebook. She had been drawing flowers like this ever since she was a child. Nothing special. Four petals. One stem. Two leaves. She traced her thumb over the little drawing as her eyes focused on a piece of lint that cluttered the hardwood floors in the distance.

A little girl raced through the meadow with a woven basket full of wildflowers. Her curls bounced effortlessly in the wind. Blue sky enveloped the landscape and her feet were caked with red dirt. She ran toward the modest stucco house ahead of her and was excited to see what was for dinner.

As she entered the house, she slowed down and her little ears picked up a sound in the distance. The sound of concerned voices muttering in the distance. Kate knew her father was sick. It was only a matter of time before the cancer came back.

Kate slid quietly through the sliding glass door and stepped into her room as she softly closed the door behind her. She gazed at her dolls and stuffed animals sternly as she tried her best to drown out the muffled sounds around her. She knelt on the floor and picked up a stuffed giraffe. Her dirt-strung legs spilled out from under her pink and white polka dot dress.

An hour later, Kate's mum lovingly called to her to come to dinner. Kate stood up, placed the giraffe back in its perfectly placed spot, wiped away any remnants of tears on her little face and stepped into the kitchen.

At dinner, Kate washed her hands like all good little girls do and took her seat at the table. She grabbed her fork of her favourite side dish and let her mind travel to far-away lands and worlds of mystery. This was the way she spent every dinner. This was the way in which she had learned to become perfect.

"And what is the purpose of Savasana in yoga class?" the radiant woman asked the class.

Kate lifted her hand to answer the question. "To be reborn," she replied.

"Yes. And what else?" The teacher moved on.

Kate glanced back to her notebook as a single tear fell onto the middle of the page.

Chapter 4
Fathers and Daughters

The next morning, Kate arrived back at the Harvest Cafe. 7.03 a.m. Three minutes late. She would really try to focus more on being punctual. As she slid behind the counter and tied her blue apron behind her back, she could not shake a feeling of grief within her. The lecture the night before had forced Kate to travel to places in her mind that she hadn't been to in quite a long time.

Kate stepped up to the register to greet a man in his early 30s. He was handsome. Blond. Green eyes. Slightly balding forehead. He wore a grey suit and black tie.

He most likely came from the legal offices down the street. As Kate arrived at the register, she took note of a detail she hadn't caught before. This man had a daughter.

A young girl who couldn't have been more than eight years old looked back at Kate from below the counter with big blue eyes. Her straight blonde hair was sticking up in a few places. She wore a green t-shirt with Tinkerbell on it.

"Two blueberry muffins and the largest coffee you've got." The man chuckled and gazed towards his daughter as if to signal to Kate, "Please help!" The exhaustion was apparent in his eyes.

Kate smiled warmly back at the man. "Ten seventy-five." She walked to the pastry case to grab their muffins and made sure to choose the biggest and prettiest muffin with the most blueberries on it for the little girl.

As Kate handed the muffins and coffee to the man, she smiled at the little girl. "I love Tinkerbell too." Kate beamed at her.

"I want to shine bright just like her when I grow up!" the little girl exclaimed.

"You will!" Kate said. "You definitely will," she repeated to herself this time as she walked away.

Kate turned to the sink of dishes for a welcome break from the customers. A single tear released out of her right eye onto the sink. The little girl had struck a chord somewhere deep within her. She too had enjoyed blueberry muffins with her own father once upon a time in an alternate universe.

Kate's father had passed away back when Kate was in college. Her internal clock did a quick calculation that took her speeding past all of the ways in which she had transformed within the last few years. Kate thought about what she would do in order to have a father with green eyes the way that little girl did. She shuddered and turned to meet the next ravenous customer at the register in front of her.

That night, Kate couldn't shake the feeling that had hung over her all day at the cafe. She pulled on sweatpants and a fluffy white sweatshirt and closed her door so that she could be alone. As she lay on her bed in the dark, she allowed herself to time travel back to her sixteen-year-old self, living in a small quintessential town.

Kate arrived at first period at 8.05 a.m. Five minutes late. She gave an apologetic smile to her art teacher and slid behind the work station to get started on her latest project. She was no good at drawing but it thrilled her simply to take part in something creative. Something that did not involve equations or diagrams or sentence frames.

At sixteen, Kate looked similar to her twenty-two-year-old self. She was skinnier, lankier and hadn't quite filled out all of her curves yet but she was still beautiful in a traditional kind of way. Her hair was blonder with a tint of brass—the result of the at-home hair lightener she used as often as she could. Small red dots trickled along her forehead, jaw and upper lip speckled with the type of acne that all teenagers had to go through at age sixteen. Her American Eagle jeans were almost the latest style and her blue navy sweater made her feel good in her own skin. The only problem was at sixteen, her own skin seemed to be changing more quickly than she could keep up with.

Kate's friend Amy glanced her way. "Everything OK?" she asked.

Kate seemed a little off to her.

"Yeah. I'm cool. Just freaking out about the winter formal."

The sentence launched Amy into an hour-long conversation about who was going to the dance with whom, what prom-posals had occurred and the latest winter fashions she had seen in Seventeen *magazine.*

This was, in fact, exactly what Kate had wanted to happen. Anything to distract from what was really going on inside her. The truth was that Kate was still shaken up to her core. Her family life had always been messy at best, but she had received some earth-shattering news the weekend prior. The cancer was back. This time, it was bad.

Kate brushed a green leaf onto her canvas as Amy brought up James. He was Kate's ultimate crush. A total bad boy. James was a year older than her and they had gone on two dates.

"I heard he was going to ask Kayli to the formal." Amy scoffed as she did her best-friend duty with diligence.

"Yeah," Kate replied. "The word on the street is that they are planning to hook up afterwards." She kept her eye on the brush the entire time.

Chapter 5
Rose-Coloured Glasses

Kate used pink tongs to grab a blueberry muffin out of a box and place it into the glass multi-tiered pastry case. The muffin top broke off halfway in the air and flew off the tongs.

"Fuck," she muttered under her breath as she tried to arrange the case to avoid the broken pastry.

Kate found Dan and asked him for her tips for the week. He obliged and she stuck the rumpled wad of cash into the back pocket of her jeans and internally calculated if it would cover her groceries and the emergency contraceptive she needed to purchase after her shift was over. It was just a precaution. She had been safe but she liked to take it anyway, just to cover all of her bases.

Kate turned and dropped her jaw as she saw a tall ghastly woman clothed in frothy pink fabric stride through the door. It was the restaurant owner, Beth. She was a real piece of work, and Kate meant that in the sincerest of ways. Beth owned the Harvest Cafe. She came from money (to be expected) and had a long family history of owning businesses in San Diego. Beth had decided in recent years to go to culinary school. The Harvest Cafe was her little 'experiment'.

Beth had a raging cougar sort of vibe going on. She was dominant. You had to be a submissive in order to survive this place. Especially if you were a female. Certainly, if you were a female that looked like Kate.

"Who broke the pastry?" Beth moaned dramatically.

Kate darted her eyes away as Beth glared at the workers one by one. "This is not the way things are supposed to be done."

Dan, smiling, walked over to comfort Beth and put two large hands around her shoulders.

A few gentle compliments allowed Beth's tantrum to release and put her ego back on track. Dan always knew how to make Beth feel better. Kate knew that Dan was a talented manager, but at that moment, she could only think about the fact that all of the managers at the Harvest Cafe were of the Y chromosome variation.

After work, Kate drove to the grocery store in the town over. She carefully stocked her cart with everyday items; bread, apples, almond milk. Enough to release any suspicion. She darted her eyes to the aisle with the 'delicates'. When the coast was clear, she quickly reached her arm for the little white box she needed and placed it under the loaf of bread.

In the car, Kate slid the little white box into her purse and pulled the zipper shut. She casually entered her apartment and called out to Zoe. No one home. She must be at Joe's.

Kate took her time in the shower. She made sure to shave every last hair on her legs before reluctantly leaving the wet oasis. She dressed calmly and rationally, putting one item of clothing on at a time as she maintained eye contact with herself in the mirror.

Kate turned on the faucet tap and filled a glass with water. She ripped open the white box and popped the baby pill onto her tongue.

"Don't look at me like that," she spoke to the mirror.

She carefully wrapped the empty box in half a roll of toilet paper and shoved it to the bottom of the basket.

An hour later, some nausea hit Kate. She winced and slid down the wall behind her. Laying on the floor of her bedroom, she was confronted with a memory that she had never wanted but was forced to keep all the same.

This memory was physical. Like the sensation of a knife stabbing her insides. A blood-curdling scream came inside of her. The feeling of a younger Kate who was lying on a cold, wet floor, alone, wondering what had just happened to her.

As quickly as the memory came through to her, it was gone. Only five minutes of time had passed in reality, yet to Kate, each second felt like it took a lifetime to move on from. She could never control when the memories showed up. They arrived fast and in the most inconvenient of times. Sometimes, they would pass quickly. Other times, she would spend days curled up in her bed alone. Tonight, she passed out, exhausted from an entire day of holding up the facade that she was thriving in this cold, dark world.

Chapter 6
The Past

Twenty-year-old Kate stared at herself in the full-length mirror and studied her outfit. She was wearing cherry red, the colour of her local university, and today was graduation day. She placed her cap on top of her head and straightened the corner of the diamond-shaped top. The tassel dangled next to a dark blonde curl. Kate had studied science over the past four years. Cum Laude. Good. Not as good as she had hoped. But good enough.

Kate pushed one chunky-heeled foot against the gas pedal of her CRV as she drove towards the university. As she got out of the car, the chill of the New Mexican spring wind caught her gown. Her cap flew away and tumbled like a weed across the parking lot.

Kate sprinted as fast as she could in her heels. As she leaned down to pick up her cap, something caught her eye. A small yellow wildflower had popped up against a crack in the pavement. Kate grinned at the flower. Wildflowers are good luck, *she thought.* A sign that good times are ahead.

Entering the auditorium, it only took a few moments to lock eyes with Cal from across the room. He was tall, with dark curls and caramel-coloured skin that drove her wild. He had a slight gap in his teeth and wore his quintessential baseball cap on his head instead of his graduation hat.

As Cal met her halfway across the room, he swept her into his arms and buried his face in her hair. She kissed him sweetly, with a soft fire starting to churn inside of her as it always did whenever he was around. Cal brought out the most wonderful feeling in her. She loved him very much. He was her soulmate, and Kate couldn't wait to spend the rest of her life with him.

After graduation and dinner at a local favourite spot with their families, Kate and Cal arrived at their new apartment. They had just decided to move in with one another and Kate practically squealed with excitement every time she thought about it. She had never lived with a boy before. A man. Cal was six years older than her and definitely not a boy like some of the guys that she had gone to school with.

Cal jiggled the key into the lock to apartment 108 and let the door swing open. He scooped Kate up into his arms and carried her into the hallway, her high heels dangling off of her feet. They both giggled and laughed uncontrollably with an easy feeling as one shoe slipped off her foot and created a loud THUD onto the carpet.

Cal didn't stop at the living room. He carried Kate straight through the hall, past the living room and delicately delivered her to the bed. He leaned down to kiss her and she could see her entire life flash before her eyes in a single moment. Things felt easy with Cal, Kate thought. How quickly she had fallen in love with this country boy. She knew her life would never be the same.

The next morning, Cal woke before Kate and slipped into the kitchen to start breakfast. Kate woke up a few minutes later and sighed contentedly to herself as the light poured into the bedroom and their kitten played on the rug. Could life get any better than this? She felt that this was truly one of those moments where if she had the power to stop her life in its tracks right then and there, she would have. She would freeze this moment and just live here forever because it was all she would ever need.

Kate pulled Cal's sweatshirt over her purple silk nightgown and glanced into the mirror at herself. Her curls bounced in a way that sung the praises of all that had transpired the night before. The universe loved them together, she thought to herself.

Kate walked quietly to the kitchen where Cal was making pancakes and she heard the hum of Johnny Cash sweetly billowing out of the speaker in the corner. Cal was an artist. He had a broody side to him, for sure, but it was just part of what made him so beautiful and special to her.

Cal seemed unaware of Kate as she arrived into the kitchen. She quietly wrapped her arms around his centre and placed her hands on his chest while nuzzling her curls into the perfect nook on his back. It was an unspoken moment of love between them. No words needed to be said. They could feel all that they needed to know. Cal handed Kate a blue plate with two pancakes on it and she smiled at him as she poured a lake of syrup onto the plate and took a giant bite.

Chapter 7
Deep Breaths

The past few years had not been easy for Kate. After her dad's cancer diagnosis, a fog had set over her teenage years. She spent long days at school and filled her afternoons with social activities, clubs and sports. She was the captain of the soccer team, the homecoming queen and the student council president, and yet, nothing could take away from the fact that she would be fatherless in a short matter of time.

At home, Kate's family worked the same strategy. Her dad went on with his life. They all did, in fact. They acted as if there had been no life-threatening diagnosis at all. Kate's dad would go to work every day at his nine-to-five job and make it home in time for supper. Kate's mum would cook and clean and call her friends on the phone. Day and night, the fog remained the same. Reality only settled in when it was completely unavoidable. Her father's health was slowly yet undeniably declining.

All the while, Kate's fast-paced life continued to move forward. She was in college now. So, Kate did all of the things that normal college students do. She attended raging parties with kegs of beer, got mixed up with frat boys that were nothing but trouble and generally was up to no good in the most innocent of ways.

When Kate got the call that her father was in the hospital, she had been up all night studying for Calculus the next day. Kate stood up from the table and allowed her eyes to gloss over as she prepared herself for this inevitable moment.

She assumed the rigid trance that she had trained herself to assume at a moment's notice. Kate slipped one black glitter ballet flat over each foot. She made sure to pull the ribbon a little tighter in order to create the perfect bow on each shoe. Kate ran her hands along her skirt to release any wrinkles. She tugged her white blouse over her rib cage. She touched a hand to her turquoise necklace and pressed a curl behind her ear.

On the drive to the hospital, Kate did not touch the radio. She didn't even turn her head to the right or left. She kept her hands at ten and two and focused extra carefully on her defensive driving skills. As she turned into the hospital, she parked perfectly centred between the two parallel white lines of the most perfectly placed parking spot and turned off the CRV's engine. Kate paused for just a moment in order to gather her thoughts, just long enough to focus, but not long enough to truly process what was happening.

Kate walked through the hallway towards her father's hospice room and noticed the vivid green colour of the scrubs the nurses and doctors were wearing. They didn't seem to notice her as much as she was noticing them. It seemed strange to her, sickly almost, and she chuckled darkly at the irony of it all.

When Kate entered room 201, her mother was already there. She was stone-faced but softly crying. Kate hugged her mother and tried to remain her rock as she had always done. Kate could barely look at her father. He was already a vegetable. She could tell in the way his body moved and how his breath escaped shallowly out of his lips.

Still, Kate walked over to him and grabbed his cold hand in hers. An oxygen tube ran under his nose and an IV drip of morphine lay in the corner of the room. Tears fell from her eyes as if someone had just turned on a faucet that couldn't be shut off.

"It's OK, Dad," Kate whispered. "Godspeed."

Chapter 8
Ghosts in Rose-Coloured Lipstick

After Kate's father died, she became a shell of herself. Kate was still Kate to the outside world. Yet on the inside, she remained empty as her soul travelled someplace else. To the place where all of those who are stricken with grief seem to go. The change was palpable to Kate's friends but only in the slightest of ways. She still received good grades in school, wore her quintessential shade of rose-coloured lipstick and spent her days hanging with friends and making plans for the future.

Yet, something was fundamentally different to Kate even though she couldn't quite put her finger on it. She had lost her faith. Kate had always been a somewhat spiritual person and she certainly had been labelled a hopeless romantic. However, Kate had felt nothing since her father had died. No signs. No messages. Just a dull, aching pain in her heart that never seemed to go away.

To fill this void, Kate started to party. She hit the pipe a little bit harder than before when her friends were smoking weed together in a circle. She made it to class but only when she filled her water bottle with pre-

mixed margaritas. She opened herself up to whomever wanted a piece of her body.

Kate might as well have tattooed the word 'vacancy' all over her body, but that would have been too obvious. Kate saw no problem with any of these things. She told herself it gave her an edge. That the others just didn't understand. They hadn't been through what she had been through. Who were they to judge?

It was a miracle that Kate found Cal. He was different from any other man. He looked at her in a way that felt like he really saw her down to her core. As if she truly mattered in the world. He looked at her this way because he really felt that for her, and Kate felt that for him too. Cal became the one bright shining ray in the fucking shitstorm that had become Kate's Junior year of college.

Cal and Kate hardly fought. Their entire relationship felt nourishing. Cleansing. Healing. Destined to be. It seemed only natural that they would live out their entire lives together. She loved him, and he loved her, so why would they not end up together?

It wasn't until Kate had uttered that one fated sentence that her entire world decided to shift out from underneath her at a moment's notice.

"I want to go to California."

Kate had always dreamt of living near the ocean. Ever since she was a little girl and she first stuck her feet in the salt water, she knew that she was meant to live her life at the beach. She would play for hours in the waves, patiently jumping and shrieking with glee at each wave that passed from underneath her.

She felt so natural in the ocean, like she was coming home to a place that she had always known. In the desert, Kate felt like a fish out of water. She needed the coastline. It was in her blood to experience it. Kate's entire family had lived on the East Coast until her father came to settle in New Mexico. Her ancestors had been islanders on the shores of the Azores islands off of Europe.

Cal, on the other hand, hated big cities. Even the word California sent shivers down his spine. He had always been a country boy. That was in his blood. It was who he had always been. Couldn't Kate see that about him? It was unfair of her to ask him to leave everything he had ever known and always wanted. Cal wanted to settle down in New Mexico. To stay true to his roots and start a family with Kate. They would get good jobs and have two children. Life would be simple and easy and beautiful as it had always been for them. As it should be for them.

The two had discussed the idea quickly and as fast as it had come up, it disappeared at exactly the same pace. Yet, Kate couldn't get the idea of California out of her mind. It was as if a seed had been planted within her that was ready to bloom. She knew deep down inside of herself that she had to go. That she would never forgive herself if she did not. That California was her destiny.

This desire seemed to reside just next to the internal fire that burned constantly for Cal. Kate put the thought out of her mind. It would all get figured out. All of the details. It would all get figured out in perfect timing, as everything always did. Still, Kate knew deep down in her gut that something big had begun to shift within her life.

Chapter 9
The Golden State

Kate and Cal began to do something they hadn't before: fight. They fought all of the time. They fought before breakfast, they fought after their favourite tv show, they fought when they were too tired to fight any more. It wasn't that they wanted to argue. It was more that it seemed that their lucky streak had run out.

Perhaps their love had been too beautiful, too rare, and so it must go away eventually. It was like lunch money. You got a certain amount. And if you wanted to buy the fancy cookies and a drink at school on Monday, you had less money for the rest of the week. That was the way it worked. The way in which the laws of the universe seemed to work. And it seemed that Kate and Cal had already spent their entire weeks' worth of lunch money within a single day.

There was also something palpably different in Cal to Kate. He was still the same Cal on the outside, but on the inside, there was a new anger, an irritability, that hadn't been there before. Cal had warned Kate that he had struggled with mental illness in his past but she had never seen it before. He had always been so sweet and protective of Kate. Cal was there to soothe her when she needed it and he had always been her best friend. Yet, here it was. This cold, mean Cal and Kate had nowhere to run from it.

After months of a stalemate, Kate received her sign from the universe in the form of a job offer. Her dream job. The location? San Diego, California. The couple finally came to a decision that they would move to California together. Kate would go out first to look for an apartment and get settled and Cal would follow her shortly when his own work was done.

Kate was secretly doing backflips in her stomach. She couldn't believe this was real. That her entire life, well, her entire adult life, she had dreamt of moving to California and now it was finally time to go. With her dream man by her side.

Two weeks later, Kate pulled a stripe of tape across the last of several cardboard boxes holding the remnants of her first twenty-two years of life. She had lovingly crammed every piece of paper and every plate with an almost hungry feeling to take her old life with her onto this new adventure. Things would be the same. Just in a different place, she consoled herself.

Kate had never lived anywhere besides New Mexico. She had studied abroad for a few months and had taken long trips here and there but always had a place to come home to. This time, things felt different for her. It was as if she could feel this giant undercurrent of her life shift in that one single moment as she closed up the last cardboard box.

Kate wiped a bead of sweat away from her brow and rose to her feet. One by one, she arranged the boxes into her CRV. Cal would come to California next week with the furniture but she had all that she would need until then.

On the day of her departure, Kate and Cal lingered outside of the blue CRV door. Even here, there was tenderness. Even here, they could communicate without words. Had Kate known how much things would have already shifted by the time she saw him next, she would have squeezed him a little bit tighter than she already did. As Kate drove out of the apartment complex with both excitement and grief in her heart, the soundtrack of Fleetwood Mac flooded the driver's seat. She caught Cal's eye in her rear-view mirror and noticed the curls that snuck out from his ball cap.

On the road, Kate stopped just an hour outside of Albuquerque. She pulled through the nearest driveway and ordered a strawberry milkshake. This is really happening, *she thought to herself as she punched the plastic straw through the cup and slurped up the milkshake. The complete magic and yet complete awfulness of it all created a feeling inside of her that she had never experienced before in her twenty-two years of life.*

Eight hours of cacti and desert later, Kate arrived at her stop for the night: a super sketchy hotel in Phoenix. Two stars. Cheap enough. Kate wondered if sleeping in her car would have been a better choice. She grabbed her purse and gingerly stepped through the red and gold carpeted halls. She held her breath until she touched the plastic key to her room and opened the door. Kate quickly slammed the door and took a breath. She could hear everything around her through the paper-thin walls, but she figured as long as she was inside of the room, she was safe.

A few fitful hours of sleep later, Kate woke to meet the sunrise. She arrived on the road early and continued her journey driving through even more cacti and dirt. Later that day, Kate arrived on the outskirts of Los Angeles. The 'Valley'. She was overwhelmed. There were more people in this little area than in her entire home state. In New Mexico, her childhood home had three acres of land. Here, she could see thousands of tiny specs of human beings surrounding the horizon for miles and miles.

We are definitely not in New Mexico any more, *Kate thought to herself.*

Around four p.m., Kate was nearing her campsite for the night. She was getting sleepy. She had never driven this far before, and suppressed a big yawn as she switched the radio on to hear Destiny's Child flood throughout the inside of the vehicle:

"Thought I couldn't breathe without you
I'm inhaling
You thought I couldn't see without you
Perfect vision
You thought I couldn't last without you

But I'm lastin'
You thought that I would die without you
But I'm livin'…"

Kate pushed the radio off and quickly rounded a corner of Highway 101. She gasped with delight as she noticed a shimmering blue mass of water in front of her. THE PACIFIC OCEAN! She had made it!

Kate navigated her GPS to the nearest beach and pulled off the highway into a neighbourhood filled with gorgeous, million-dollar homes. She slowed and parked the car, stretching her arms overhead as she arrived. Kate saw a huge wooden staircase leading from a cliff to the ocean far below in front of her. Green shrubbery surrounded Kate and for just a moment, she was all alone. Just Kate, the blue sky and the sparkling ocean that she had given up all of her old dreams for.

THE PACFIC OCEAN! WE MADE IT! Kate was enthralled. She sat for a moment to take it all in. Tears rolled down her cheeks. I really did it, Kate thought. It dawned on her that she was thrilled to be there by herself.

"No matter what happens, I did this," Kate said to herself. She knew that this moment would live on in her heart for the remainder of her life as the day that she fulfilled her lifelong dream of moving to California.

After snapping a quick selfie to remember the moment, Kate succumbed to the feelings of hunger and exhaustion that overwhelmed her. She was camping tonight, the cheapest and easiest option, although in

California even camping still seemed to be expensive. Kate arrived at her campsite, number 33, and began to set up her tent.

She knew what she was doing when it came to this sort of stuff. Kate had been on tons of backpacking trips throughout the New Mexican backcountry with her father in her younger years. She pitched the tent and used a rock to hammer the metal spikes into the ground, being sure to avoid the harder areas as she had been taught to do. Kate pulled out a bag of instant rice and lit the flame to the camp stove that had once belonged to her father.

A few minutes later, Kate pulled out her journal and slipped on a sweatshirt as the sun started to set. Savouring one metallic bite of rice at a time, Kate relished in the moment. As darkness fell, she cleaned up and slid into her tent. A feeling of sweet aloneness followed her. This is exciting, *Kate thought. She pulled out two pieces of computer paper and grinned ear to ear. Her offer letter. A coyote howled in the distance and Kate shivered, suddenly aware of just how alone she was in that moment. She clicked off her headlamp and fell into a fitful sleep.*

The next morning, Kate rose with the sun. Her tent was already getting stuffy and hot at seven a.m. She packed everything up and shoved it into the trunk of her car and drove two hours south to San Diego. As she drove on the 5, she giggled with happiness at the sparkling blue water on her right. White cars sped past her and weaved in and out of traffic in much too tight spaces. A text from her sister popped up on the dashboard of her phone. "You are NEVER coming home." *She had laughed over text after receiving a photo of the ocean from Kate.*

When Kate arrived on the outskirts of San Diego, she felt a shiver go up and down her spine. This was really it. She drove into the main area of the city and only then did it dawn on her that she had no idea where to go next. Kate hadn't really planned what to do once she arrived. She had focused only on making it there.

Kate pulled off the interstate and entered the parking lot of a Starbucks. After grabbing a large iced americano, she googled local hostels. As she sipped the cold, sweet liquid, the realisation of what she had just done started to settle in. She was alone. Like, completely alone. On an alien planet where all of the people looked like movie stars and perfect weather was non-negotiable. Kate pulled out her phone and wrote a text message to Cal. "Here, babe. You're going to LOVE it!"

Chapter 10
Studio Apartments

Kate spent the next morning drinking coffee outside on the balcony of her hostel. There was a view of the San Diego Harbour and Kate was thrilled about it. The palm trees swayed in the balmy breeze and the Pacific Ocean sparkled almost as if it was whispering to her, "I'm so happy you are here."

Kate pulled out her laptop and opened up Craigslist. The weight of the mountain that was ahead of her started to settle in and she could feel the emotions dim around her a little. Except for the last few days, she had only been to California for a weekend road trip. She didn't really know anything about how to live in a major city and she definitely didn't know how to navigate it all alone.

There were almost no listings online that she could afford. Kate was working for a non-profit organisation and Cal would need to find a new job once he transferred out to San Diego. Finally, she landed on a somewhat affordable listing near the beach and put the address into her phone. As she pulled to the side of the street and parked her CRV, she saw a building that matched the listing online. It looked so cute! She could totally see herself and Cal thriving there.

Kate stepped out onto the sidewalk and grabbed the application for the apartment. As she walked around the corner, she noticed a long line of people. What could they all be waiting for? A sinking feeling landed in the pit of her stomach, as she realised they were all in line for the apartment. Ahead of her.

Kate didn't even bother to put her application in. After several failed attempts to find an apartment, she finally settled for a sublease of a tiny 350-square-foot apartment in the urban centre of the city. She walked up the stairs alone and stepped through the door.

She didn't have far to go. The studio apartment was smaller than a basic hotel room. As she sat on the floor, she pulled out her phone to FaceTime Cal but got his voicemail instead. She rolled out her sleeping bag, turned off the light and fell into a fitful sleep.

The next morning, Kate decided to go to the beach. She had no idea where to go so she pulled out her phone and navigated to the closest access. Her GPS took her to a sprawling wide beach that seemed to go on for miles and miles. This place was different from the beaches she had grown fond of in her childhood. Most things were different here, she thought.

Kate couldn't quite describe in words what it felt like to be in California. It was beautiful here, that was a given. People had been mostly nice to her. The food was good and the weather was beautiful. Yet, she *couldn't quite put her finger on what was feeling off to her. It was colder here, somehow, she thought.*

Kate wandered to the edge of the beach where the dogs were. She plopped down on a blanket and wrapped her hands around her denim jacket. As Kate sat by herself watching the dogs, she felt a calming presence surrounding her. She had never seen such joy as she did now on both the dogs' and their owners' faces. This feeling, this freedom, she realised, was what she had journeyed to California for.

Chapter 11
Broken Dishes and Christmas Wishes

Kate pulled a frothy beverage from Dan's hands and placed a plastic lid securely on top. She turned around to hand the drink to a beautiful family of four. Dan was finishing up the touches on their miniature hot chocolates.

Not much had changed at the Harvest Cafe over the last few months. The main difference was that it was Christmas-time. Kate's outfit didn't change, the pink decor remained just as nauseating as it had been, and the customers seemed to be just as glamorous. Even the California weather remained a wonderful seventy-two degrees. The amazing weather and balmy breeze set the perfect backdrop for the quintessential cafe and its daily offering.

For Kate, only a few things had changed as well since the month of October. She had not had any more contact with Zach after their one drunken encounter together. Zoe had returned to Los Angeles for a few weeks in order to enjoy the Christmas season with her family and Joe. Kate herself would be flying home to New Mexico in another week for a few days to celebrate with her family.

Kate wasn't quite sure how she felt about her trip. She deeply missed the scents and images of home; roasting green chiles, sugar cookies warming in the oven, the dark night sky with a thousand twinkling stars and the huge Christmas tree that her family always placed in their living room each December.

As Kate glanced out of the open French doors to the café, she smiled to herself. It wasn't all bad here. The ocean sparkled back at her and seemed to wink and say hello. She had lived in California for almost five months and she still wasn't sure how she felt about it. Things had been challenging for her here. Back home, she had always remained popular and she never had any trouble making friends. But here, things felt a little bit different.

Certainly, a part of that feeling probably had to do with the breakup with Cal. He had broken up with her not more than a week after he came out and saw the studio apartment. She also hadn't lasted long at her non-profit job that she had come out here for in the first place. It wasn't a good fit. Yet, shouldn't things be easier if she was destined to make it in California?

Kate couldn't help but wonder in the back of her mind if she had made the wrong decision. Maybe she wasn't cut out for California after all. She missed the open spaces and vast wilderness that was so common in New Mexico. Perhaps Cal had been right about California. What if she had made the wrong decision to stay?

Kate was rudely awakened from her daydreaming by an angry Beth strutting through the door in tight leather leggings and an extravagant peach coat. Beth gave Kate a single disapproving glance as she sauntered to the back of the restaurant and pushed through the kitchen doors.

Kate let a soft breath escape from her lips. She had survived the wrath of Beth, for the time being that was. She gave a subtle glance through the kitchen doors and noticed the cook taking a beating about the state of the bean sprouts in the avocado toast. Kate allowed her eyes to wander for a moment behind the cook to a younger man that was patiently chopping onions and pretending not to hear the conversation that was taking place.

The cooks in the kitchen were all super handsome and a major incentive for Kate to continue this stupid job. They didn't speak English very well but that didn't matter to her. Every few minutes or so, Kate would glance through the plexiglass doors and lock eyes with one of them for a split second. She never ended up having a conversation with one of them that was not food-related, but she liked to think that they also pondered about what it would feel like to have dinner with her at this very cafe on a Saturday evening.

Kate pushed through the kitchen doors and went out to explore the cafe lobby. She began to collect plates and cups from the countertops and wiped the empty tables down with a pink terry cloth towel. Kate was jittery from too many espresso shots and the general uneasiness that seemed to naturally arrive with Beth's presence.

As Kate carried a stack of dirty white dishes in her arms, she kicked open the door to the kitchen and immediately heard a loud *THUD* clash back at her as the dishes flailed from her arms and threw shards of broken glass everywhere.

Someone had left a delivery box near the inside of the cafe door and Kate had not been able to see it. None of that mattered now though. She had royally fucked up. Kate could see Beth mentally taking notes on her and placing the debacle neatly into the filing cabinet that she kept for all of her employees in her head.

Beth already didn't like Kate. They began on good terms but things started to go south after Kate had noticed the ways in which all women were treated in the cafe. To Kate, she was taking a stand for women everywhere by maintaining a mildly salty presence around Beth at all times.

Kate knew that when the new schedule came out on Friday, she would have a few changes to hers. It always worked this way. If you messed up, you lost hours. Especially if the person who messed up happened to look like Kate.

Chapter 12
Graduation Night

Kate walked out of the cafe doors and shivered as she wrapped her jacket tightly around her chest. It was chilly for a San Diego night and almost felt like a real winter evening to her. Kate was deep in thought about the events that had played out at the cafe earlier that day. She nervously wondered how long she would be able to keep up this stunt. Each day got worse and worse at the cafe as time went on.

Meanwhile, Kate's yoga practice was getting stronger. Tonight, she was graduating from teacher training and shortly after that were try-outs for her local yoga studio. If Kate could land a teaching position, she would be able to cut down her hours at the cafe. It still wouldn't be enough money to completely quit her job but she would have to spend less time at the cafe. It would be a really good start.

Kate gasped as she heard a man's voice shouting behind her. "Kate! Kate!" The man was jogging down the sidewalk towards her. She recognised this man as a customer that she had served in the cafe just before she clocked out. The man was incredibly handsome. She could already tell from looking at him that he was different from any man that she had ever been with before.

"Hey." The man was a little out of breath after jogging. "I'm Duke." He straightened his black tie against his neck as he spoke. Her eyes wandered to his throat. His Adam's apple protruded from the centre of his throat and thick droplets of scruff decorated the sides of his jaw. His dark brown eyes lay underneath heavy-set brows. The man's eyelashes were thick and long and did that thing that no girl could ever seem to replicate for their own lashes, no matter how much money they spent trying.

"Hey." Kate met his eyes with a guarded glance and wrapped her jacket tightly around her chest.

"You're really beautiful," he said.

"Umm, thanks." Kate awkwardly acknowledged him.

"I'd like to take you out. To your favourite restaurant. Maybe see the ocean after?"

Kate's eyes travelled over the man. He was older than her. Definitely in his thirties. He certainly was rich, she observed, and contemplated his Cartier cufflinks and perfectly polished black shiny shoes.

"Yeah, OK, I guess," Kate stammered. She was taken aback by this man. What did he want to do with her? Guys like this ended up with girls like *her* (Kate glanced over towards a tall, thin woman ordering avocado toast from the cafe window). The man grinned and got her number. She gave him a half smile in spite of herself and turned to walk away.

"Night." Kate turned on her heels and walked toward her CRV. Her eyes widened now that he couldn't see her. Unexpected.

Chapter 13
Blue Leggings

Later that evening, Kate arrived at her yoga studio for graduation night. She had decided to rock electric blue leggings tonight with a black sweater. As Kate walked up to the studio doors, the vibrant colour of her leggings caught her eye and a memory flashed through her internal world.

Eighteen-year-old Kate stepped into her first yoga class in her college gym. The teacher was a glistening Indian woman wearing bright blue leggings. She looked fierce to Kate. Strong. Grounded. Stable. She didn't care what anyone thought of her. Kate wished at that moment that she could be a yoga teacher, too. She wished she had enough confidence to rock blue leggings.

Kate looked down at herself and laughed out loud into the empty air. She was now the woman that her younger self had one day dreamt of being. She was working to become the fierce and confident woman she had once so greatly admired and observed within someone else.

Kate and her friends squealed and screamed with excitement that this was their final night of training.

Tonight, they would be teaching a yoga class to friends and family. Each girl nervously recited their part to the others. The jitters felt throughout the room were palpable.

As Kate flowed through down dogs and halfway lifts, she felt a warm peaceful feeling begin to come over her. She could not believe that she had really made it here. To this moment.

Kate's part would be the very last teacher to speak in the class tonight. As time ran out and Kate got closer to her yoga debut, she started to feel nerves roll like waves underneath her skin. She stood up and nervously walked to the back of the room, brushing her hands over her ribcage to smooth out her top. She winced as she spoke to the quiet room at first. But once she heard her voice ripple throughout the room, she was pleasantly surprised by how gracefully it came out.

As Kate began to walk around the room, she felt her confidence build. A smile came to her lips. She could see that smile flow out into the crowded room to every practitioner. The students rose from their final posture and came to a seat as Kate sat cross-legged facing the students in front of her. With her eyes closed, she pressed her hands against her heart and felt a flutter of feelings rush across her chest.

After saying the final closing, Kate opened her eyes and faced the room. "Thank you so much for coming. Thank you for giving us this opportunity to be reborn." She smiled at her instructor in the front row and the crowd burst into applause. Kate's fellow teachers came to squish her in the middle of a giant embrace. Kate felt as if she were in one of those sports movies and had just scored the winning goal that would take the team on to the finals.

As Kate drove home that evening, she felt a trickle of warm salty water gush beneath her lashes. Mascara rolled down her cheeks and the radio hummed a Johnny Cash song. She couldn't quite put her finger on the description of what she was feeling. Tired. Exhausted. Alone. Yet proud. So proud. Of herself, her ability to weather the challenges that came up in her life and to withstand the undeniable changes that were inevitably beginning to blossom within herself.

Chapter 14
The Taco Stand

Zoe lay on the corner of Kate's bed, grinning up at her.

"OK. Who is this guy again?" Zoe smirked.

"Just some guy. I don't know. He goes to the coffee shop, I guess," Kate stammered and stuttered as she rummaged through her closet.

"He sounds rich. Rich guys always expect something," Zoe said.

"I can handle it, Zo," Kate replied. "What about this?" She hung up a pale pink dress in front of her friend.

"Yeah, that's good." Zoe pulled out her phone and started typing away, unconcerned with the state of Kate's future romantic life.

An hour later, a knock came at their front door. Kate opened the door to see a shivering Duke holding a dozen pink roses. Kate smiled, grabbed the roses and went to find a vase for them in the kitchen. As Duke stepped into the modest apartment, he glanced around to the left and right.

"It's not much…" Kate started to explain.

"It's awesome," Duke said. "I used to live around this area a few years ago."

Duke opened the door to his black BMW and Kate felt completely out of place. Her outside appearance mimicked what she thought that people with money acted like but on the inside, she was squirming with discomfort. Why was he into her? She didn't get it.

"You look really beautiful." Duke gazed at Kate warmly. "Where do you want to go eat?"

"There's a really great taco shop over on Mission."

"A taco shop? That's where you want to eat?" Duke seemed surprised.

"Yeah. It's amazing," Kate said.

"We can go anywhere, you know." Duke smiled at her.

"Yeah, I know." She smiled back. "And I think you could use some tacos."

Duke laughed and seemed entertained. No girls in his neighbourhood or near his age range would ever settle for that. They all wanted to go to the most exquisite dining areas with the latest trendy foods. They didn't eat gluten or dairy or meat. Kate was completely different from them.

They rolled up to the little beach shack and saw less than five cars surrounding the restaurant. The couple walked through the front doors and were met with brightly coloured lights and smiling faces. Kate ordered for the two of them and they walked over to a little aluminium table in the far-off corner. Mariachi music blared from the speakers as they made small talk with one another.

They talked about jobs and exes and hopes for the future. The conversation flowed naturally despite the fact that they were complete strangers a few days ago. Kate dipped a tortilla chip into the bright red dish of salsa and grinned at Duke trying to eat a carne asada taco.

"When did you get so wound up?" she pried at him. "Have you always been this way?"

"Actually, no," he spoke to her as he looked down at his blue shirt and wiped a spot of spilled salsa with a napkin. She laughed in delight. "I used to be just like you. A long time ago."

After dinner, they drove in his car to the sunset. Kate showed him a secret spot to pull off the side of the road where they could be alone with the palm trees and waves in front of them. She glanced over at the driver's seat and really took a look at this man in the dim evening light. He was really gorgeous. She caught his eye and felt the best kind of shiver run down her spine.

The couple watched the sun fall beneath the clouds and the whole scene in front of them took on a fiery shade of golden orange. It was breath-taking. An indie song played softly on the radio and added to the ethereal ambience.

Duke grabbed Kate's hand which had been resting on the centre console. She looked at him, surprised for a moment, and then intertwined each of her fingers deep within his. Kate leaned toward Duke and smiled. In one fell swoop, Duke twisted his hand behind Kate's hair and pulled her towards him. Their lips met with ease and a slight spark. This was the start of something big, Kate just knew it.

Chapter 15
A New Beginning

The next morning, Kate awoke with a peaceful feeling in her heart. She was still flying high off of golden hour with Duke the night before. Kate felt as if a new leaf were turning for her and her journey in California. Things seemed lighter somehow.

Kate greeted Zoe in the kitchen with a big smile on her face and poured herself a giant cup of coffee. Zoe smirked.

"Looks like someone had a good night!"

"I did." Kate smiled and took a sip from the steaming mug. "Duke is so different," she gushed. "I should have started dating older men a long time ago."

Zoe laughed at Kate and thought to herself perhaps Kate was onto something.

Kate slipped into some workout clothes and tied her sneakers one at a time. Rubbing sunscreen on her face, she could see the slight glow of her skin in the mirror. As she placed her sunglasses on and stepped out of the front door, she felt fresh and light.

Kate started to jog towards the local pier. She felt the warm air on her skin and the sunshine kiss the back of her neck. It was one of those days that you would never forget, simply for the fact that it was mundane in the most exceptional of ways.

Later that day, Kate arrived at the Harvest Cafe and gushed the story of her date to Dan. "I've seen that guy in here before." Dan smirked. "I've never seen him with any girls though. He's hot." Dan gave Kate a knowing side-glance and then placed his pen back onto the accounting books to continue where he had left off. Today was Kate's last day working at the Harvest Cafe before she flew home to New Mexico for the holidays.

Kate stopped and looked around to take in all that had transpired over the last year in San Diego. Emotions flooded through her body and she struggled to sort through them one at a time as they came rushing through. First was grief, for all of the pain that she had been through. Next was struggle, life had been challenging here. Then came beauty, the rawness of it all always struck her. And finally, a newer type of feeling: lightness. It was subtle, but her life was definitely beginning to shift out of the darkness. Each day, Kate became a little more confident in herself and her path in California. She was learning how to survive here.

The next morning, Kate rolled her black suitcase up to the desk attendant at the San Diego airport. The attendant wore a red Santa hat and a smile despite the inevitable madness of holiday air travel. Kate mirrored the smile right back to the attendant. She was grateful to be on her way to see her family.

As Kate walked through the airport halls, she was struck with how much things had shifted within her. She felt at this very moment as if she were leaving her home to go visit someplace else. This was the first time that it did not feel like the situation was reversed.

As the plane rose into the clouds, Kate stared down at the beaming golden light streaming out over the Pacific Ocean and golden city. When Kate landed in Albuquerque, she felt a wave of grief overwhelm her chest like someone was sitting on it. The last time that she had flown back to New Mexico, Cal had been with her.

Kate turned her phone on and received two *dings*, meaning she had text messages. One from her mum and sister, *"We can't wait to see you!"* The other from Duke, *"Have a lovely trip. See you when you return. :)"* Kate beamed with happiness. She had a new beginning waiting for her back in California.

Chapter 16
Back Home

As Kate stepped into the Albuquerque airport, she felt the quintessential clack of her heels on the tile floor. This could only mean that she had arrived. It was cold here, a real winter, and she felt the chill in the air even being inside. Groups of bustling humans walked back and forth in between her. People looked different here than they did in California. Simpler. Older. Somewhat happier. At peace with who they were and where they were headed.

Kate stepped off the elevator and saw her family and scooped them up in a big group hug. They quickly swept up her bags and carried them to the car. As they drove to their favourite New Mexican restaurant for Christmas dinner, Kate glimpsed the snow-covered mountain range that had framed her younger years. It was beautiful, she thought, this place where she had grown up.

At dinner, Kate's family chatted and made up for lost time. They spoke of transitions and jobs and friends and the news, all the while taking sips from mugs of steaming cinnamon coffee by the fireside. The hacienda-style restaurant they were at was Kate's favourite. Kate closed her eyes and took a big breath into this very moment. She had missed this. This feeling of warmth. Connection. Simplicity. Family. Home.

Later that evening, their car slowed down as it pulled up to a gravel road. The crunch of the gravel could only signify one thing to Kate: she was home. Her boot-covered foot stepped onto the gravel and she gasped at the feeling of the bitter cold on her cheeks. Something inside of her body told her to look up. The starry night sky beamed down upon her and in an instant, she felt as small as a single ant. In the country, you could see every star in the sky. Even the big dipper. Even the milky way.

Kate pondered at the cloudy trail of dust that traced along the sky. You didn't get this feeling in Southern California. Kate felt thankful and haunted by her childhood all at once. A flash of bright orange caught Kate's eye in the sky. A shooting star. Kate gleamed and made a wish as she always did.

She could feel her dad's presence here. It felt palpable, more tangible, in the home where he had so recently lived. As Kate turned the door knob and stepped into her childhood home, she could recognise it instantly as the same place she had left one year prior.

Yet, something felt different to her. It was subtle. Something in the way a picture hung or in the feeling of a new blanket dressing the couch. Life had been lived here.

Kate set her bags down and smiled. Tomorrow was Christmas! It was her absolute favourite holiday. She picked up a ceramic reindeer and then set it back down. Images of Christmases past flooded through her brain and she realised how much she had needed to come back to this place.

Kate stared up at the dark ceiling in her bed later that night. She couldn't shake the presence of Cal. The feeling unnerved her. She had not experienced many plane rides without Cal by her side.

It seemed to her that her entire life had been lived in New Mexico with Cal. It was as if she hadn't spent two decades of her life living in this very bedroom experiencing life before she had met him. As Kate turned over to fall asleep, she caught a glimpse of the starry night sky out of her window, winced and let out a soft whimper, and fell fast asleep.

Chapter 17
Best Friends

Christmas morning was filled with cinnamon rolls, wrapping paper strewn floorboards and several cups of coffee. Kate and her sister watched Christmas movies and baked cookies all day. She loved how Christmas morning seemed to be some magical vortex in which time never passed. A place where nothing that happened on the West Coast mattered in the slightest. A place where no one cared to know about any of the drama that was happening daily at the Harvest Cafe.

Around three o'clock in the afternoon, a red car pulled into the driveway. Kate would have recognised that car anywhere. It was Jessica, Kate's best friend since the third grade. Kate beamed as she ran outside of the house and screamed with delight. The two girls ran towards one another in the front yard and jumped up and down as they embraced one another like schoolgirls.

Jessica was studying pre-med at their local college. She held a tray of baked goods in her arms along with a few wrapped gift bags. "I brought you some biscotti! My mum made them this morning."

Kate smiled. She had spent every weekend as a kid at Jessica's house and Kate had made biscotti alongside Jessica's family many times throughout the past.

The girls walked into the house and Kate's mum gave Jessica a big hug. They were all family here. They spent the rest of the evening playing board games, drinking wine and catching each other up on the updates of a small-town life. They talked about sisters and cousins. Weddings and funerals. They spoke of who graduated with what degree and what experience the neighbour's cousin had on her winter vacation to Europe. They spoke of these things because that's what you did in a small town. Your friends were your family. Your family were your friends. This was the way that it had always been and the way it always would be.

Around nine o'clock that evening, Kate went to walk Jessica to the door with gifts and cookies in hand.

"How's school?" Kate asked Jessica.

"It's good. Hard. But good," Jessica replied. "I miss you."

The girls looked at one another with big, bold, beautiful eyes with a look that could only be understood between two women who had been friends for fifteen years. Who had sleepovers every week and made hot fudge sundaes in each other's kitchens. Who stayed up until three a.m. during those sleepovers talking about their hopes and dreams, and their sorrows.

They had shaved their legs together for the first time in the bathtub at Jessica's house. They filled the tub with hot water and winced as they fumbled with their razors and created small nicks every few moments. Kate had come home sheepishly the next morning with little pieces of toilet paper stuck to her legs to cover up the cuts.

Kate's mum smiled and said, "What did you do?"

The girls embraced and said goodbye, knowing that it would probably be another year before they saw each other again.

"Come visit if you ever are around San Diego." Kate smiled at Jessica.

"I will!" she said.

Yet, they both knew that as reality set in, this would not happen. Life used to be so simple when they were kids. Now it was filled with jobs and relationships and working hard to make rent on the first of the month. They enjoyed this moment anyways and continued to move forward with their lives the way that all human beings eventually learn to do.

Chapter 18
10,000 Feet Up

Kate rested her forehead against the plane's window and felt the cool chill of an early morning flight. She sighed a deep breath and felt golden rays of sunlight shimmer into the plane's cabin from the sunrise outside. It was early. Six thirty a.m. Kate always took early flights now because they were the cheapest airfare on the local airlines.

Kate was still trying to digest the entire trip. She felt as if something deep within her had shifted but she couldn't quite put her finger on what it was. She often felt this way after going home. It allowed her to experience how much she had grown and changed in her life compared to her younger days. Kate knew that Zoe would have arrived back at their beach apartment by the time she got home and they would spend hours discussing their travels with one another over bagels and coffee.

Still, Kate felt that she needed to be with herself to move through all that had shifted within her. Her trip home had been fabulous. It felt great to see her family. It felt as though the dull ache that had constantly existed within her heart when she was away from them had finally subsided. Adulthood, Kate thought, was learning how to survive without all of the pieces of your heart in a single place.

What was particularly troubling for Kate this trip were her memories of Cal. She wished that she could say she was over him. She did lie and tell her family and her friends that she was. She had become an expert at thriving in California without him. She had a job, a spiritual practice, good friends and a genuine love for her new city. She had Duke, and before him, she had plenty of other men, too.

Still Kate could not shake the feeling that she could most accurately describe as a phantom limb sensation. As if she were moving through her life and yet in some alternate universe, there was a world in which Cal and Kate had never split up. In this universe, they had chosen the life that Cal had always wanted for them. There was a beautiful log cabin, small, yet quaint. Two children, a boy and a girl, with long curls escaping out of their winter hats as they sprinted through the snow in the front yard. A pregnant Kate, glowing even though she had gained a few pounds since the pregnancy and, truthfully, just in the years since she had become a mother. A smiling Cal, who loved her no matter what she looked like simply because she was the one that was destined for him.

Kate pondered this dream-life in her head. She wondered if it had been worth it to give it up. That life seemed easier somehow. It seemed to her as if she had taken the more difficult choice. But had she really? Kate experienced so much more self-confidence in her life after Cal left her.

By every definition of the word, she was now living her dream life. But was she really? What really mattered in life? And how did you know if you were doing it correctly? What if you lost something you had really, really wanted? But at the same time, you didn't necessarily choose to let that thing go? What if it had left you because that was the way in which it was meant to be? What if all human beings were supposed to feel this feeling regardless of having the perfect log cabin with the love of your life? Would she really be happier if she had taken the other choice?

Kate would never know. What she did know was that she enjoyed visiting this place in her head every now and again. This place that no one or nothing could ever take from her.

"Something to drink?" the flight attendant chirpily asked Kate.

"No, thank you," she replied.

Kate shook her head and took note of a fluffy white cloud outside of the plane window. She pulled out her phone and pressed play on an album that her sister had recommended. The sweet female voice serenaded her and soothed her early morning thoughts. The lyrics to the song *Emmylou* by First Aid Kit called out to her:

"When it's you I find like a ghost in my mind
I am defeated and I gladly wear the crown."

Chapter 19
End Games

Kate and Zoe wasted no time at all getting back into the normal groove of their everyday lives that January. This showed up in the simple ways in which they allowed their bodies to rest intertwined on the couch, one foot of Kate's resting easily into the crook of Zoe's knee as they watched old reruns of reality tv shows on the screen in their living room. In San Diego, they were each other's home away from home.

The lazy afternoons that they shared together were only interrupted by the need to work and, of course, when the boyfriends came calling around. Kate had begun dating Duke seriously by now. They spent evenings at his house often.

Zoe noticed the balance of nights that Kate spent at the beach apartment versus Duke's sleek northern San Diego townhouse started to dwindle as the days went on. Zoe too was beginning to deepen her relationship with Joe. It seemed a bittersweet pill, this boyfriend thing. Sooner or later, they all had to grow up and move on from their roommate days, right?

One hazy February day, Kate and Duke walked hand and hand down the rocky beach close to his home.

Valentine's Day was only a few days away and the vibe around the city seemed to ooze romance and commitment. Duke turned to look at Kate. A strand of her hair caught in the wind and she met him with her gaze.

"These past few months…" he stammered.

Kate observed this man that was before her. She could tell he was a good man. He was so different from any man she had ever been with before. He was certainly different from the hometown boys that Kate had dated back in New Mexico. She felt safe with Duke. They experienced happy moments together and smiled more often than they did not. Their sex life was good. Yet, Kate couldn't quite shake the feeling that something felt very off about the relationship. It was too fast. Too pressured. Much too serious. With Cal, she had never thought twice about what she was doing or where she was headed. But that feeling had gotten her here. And now, things were different.

Duke continued on. "I've been very lucky to have you in my life." Duke's tone was serious. "I love you, Kate." He sheepishly looked at her and she noticed a silvery stand of grey hair against his beard. Kate stood shell-shocked for a moment in the sand. The ocean crashed in celebration and met them with a wave hovering nearby.

"I love you, too," Kate whispered to Duke and tears welled up in her hazel eyes.

Kate wrapped her arms around Duke's neck and they embraced lovingly. She could feel his heart beat against her chest. She felt the nuzzle of his beard against her cheek. Kate noticed the sparkling blue ocean meeting up with the horizon behind Duke.

"And I want you to move in with me!" Duke let a single watery glance overcome him just for a moment.

Later that night, Kate took a walk at the bay by herself. Her emotions were all over the place still. She was happy, for sure. How could she not be? But she also felt a longing ache in her heart for the ways in which her life used to be so much simpler. There was no easy answer. If she moved in with Duke, she would be happy. She would also be abandoning Zoe. Kate was sure that she and Zoe would remain friends. Yet, it was inevitable that some things in their relationship would change. *Moving in with a person changes the entire track of your life,* Kate thought.

Kate wondered at that moment if adulthood was simply this. This feeling of uncertainty. All that you could do was leap and hope for the best. Would she ever be certain that anything was the right path for her? How could you really, truly know? Kate turned down the alleyway and shot a quick goodnight text to Duke.

Chapter 20
The Satisfaction of Saying No

Kate's romantic relationship was not the only thing that was quickly shifting in her life. Her yoga career had also taken off as soon as their graduation class had ended. Kate was offered a teaching role at her local studio and she seemed to be thriving there.

Kate was now teaching around ten yoga classes a week. She had the opportunity to pick up even more if she wanted to. The only problem was the Harvest Cafe. Kate really hated her job at the cafe, but it gave her the financial freedom that she needed in order to survive in California. Yoga fed her soul spiritually, but it left her wallet hanging out to dry.

Kate walked into the Harvest Cafe for yet another evening shift. The feeling of disdain that hit her whenever she walked into this place was now beginning to grow out of hand. The first few hours of Kate's shift flew by without any drama. During the third hour of Kate's time behind the counter, a middle-aged man who sat at a table with his wife and baby stepped up to the counter.

Kate turned around and saw the man holding up his dinner plate. She knew right away that this was not a good sign. Kate had trained herself over time to understand the different signs that occurred in the restaurant world. A lot of laughter from the table meant that things were good. A shake of the salt meant that the food was OK. A held-up plate at the front register? The worst omen. A customer looking for reconciliation.

"Hi! Can I help you?" Kate made sure to layer her chipper tone on extra thick (these customers were always the ones to leave a bad Yelp review that highlighted your exact facial features and terrible service).

"Yeah. I want to add asparagus to this dish."

Kate shuddered internally. Beth had asked the servers not to allow any modifications for customers. It was a ridiculous ask. Prices at the cafe were outstanding and customers deserved the omelette of their dreams if that was what they were paying for. However, what Beth said was what happened in the cafe if you wanted to keep your job.

"I'm so sorry, sir. We cannot create modifications to that dish."

What happened next created a tornado of emotion within Kate. Retelling the story later to Duke, she was unable to recount even exactly what the customer had said to her. All that she knew was that the man had started yelling at her.

Kate thought it was something about asparagus and somewhere else he had seen it on the menu. All she knew was that in her mind, she began shrinking, slowly getting smaller. Slowly succumbing to the feeling. The stabbing. The knife ripping into her. She was no longer twenty-two-year-old Kate. She was lying on the cold, wet floor, tears flowing out of her eyes as a silent scream escaped the body of a much younger Kate.

Kate's face remained mostly unaffected at the surface during the interaction. She was sure the man did not notice the slight glisten of moisture that was starting to collect at the base of her bottom lashes. Her jaw hardened as she took the plate from the customer and looked him in the eyes.

Without a smile this time, Kate turned towards the kitchen with the plate of asparagus-less dinner. She kicked open the kitchen doors, dropped the plate into the sink with a clatter and walked out the back door. She never took a second glance behind her at the wide, staring eyes of the cooks that she could feel upon her back as she went.

Chapter 21
Now What

Kate didn't stop moving once she left the back door of the Harvest Cafe. She walked calmly, at a brisk pace, towards her car down the street. Anger coursed through her veins and adrenaline pumped from the crown of her head down through each of her fingertips and out through each of her toes. Kate opened the door to her CRV, backed out of the small busy street and drove home to her beach apartment.

It was not until Kate had safely arrived in her parking spot, turned the ignition off and had safely pulled up the emergency brake until it couldn't move any more that she allowed herself to react. A blood curdling howl erupted from her body and for a moment, it scared even her, the guttural sound that her body could create. She let it release. She let the tears run as if a water faucet had been turned on at full blast from the centre of her heart.

Kate cried because of the man at the cafe who had yelled at her. But she also cried for every man that had ever chosen to leave her. To abandon her. From the boyfriend who had coerced Kate to be intimate with him when she had refused her consent to the asshole fraternity brother that had taken her virginity and then never even gave her a second thought. She cried for Cal. She cried for every one-night stand that she had since he left her that made her feel cold and empty and hollow inside.

Kate cried for the way in which she had seen other women getting yelled at. She cried for all of the women who had ever been neglected by men. Beaten. Broken. Hurt. Abandoned.

Kate cried for the way in which married men would stare at her in a public place when their wives were so obviously standing next to them. She cried for all of the stories her friends had told her about men who had hurt them physically, as if they were simply discussing the weather. She cried for all of the women that had arrived on this Earth just to run into the cold, dark shoulder of a man that they had been told would save them.

Kate didn't care that she had just left her job. She never saw any of those people around in her daily life anyways. Kate was not one of them. She pulled out her phone and typed two words onto her screen between blurry eyes and quivering fingers. Five little figures that would forever change the course of her trajectory throughout life. *"I QUIT."*

Chapter 22
Moving Day

One week later, Kate was packing her books lovingly into a cardboard box. Items were strewn all over the floor of her room. It seemed that Kate was always moving. She had lived in five different places since she first left her childhood home and moved into her first college dorm room.

Zoe had made the decision to move in with Joe after their lease ended at the beach apartment. She was also packing in the next room and shouted to Kate through their shared wall. "Why do we have so much SHIT?" an exasperated Zoe yelled through the house.

"I have NO idea!" Kate exclaimed back at her.

Kate pulled a couple of stuffed animals off of her bed. One, a stuffed brown bear with the words 'I Love You' inscribed in cursive on the front. The other, the same stuffed giraffe that little Kate had loved so much during her childhood days. Kate took the brown bear and shoved it into a bag full of trash. It had been from Cal. With the giraffe in her arms, she traced her thumb over the spot where one of its ears had been missing. Kate wrapped the giraffe in an old sweater, shoved it to the bottom of her suitcase and covered it with mountains of her other clothes.

An hour later, Duke arrived at the beach apartment. Joe was already in Zoe's room helping her pack.

"I've got the moving truck outside," Duke said to Kate as she kissed him on the cheek.

"Awesome! I'm all packed up," she said.

Duke walked into Kate's room and grabbed three boxes and hoisted them up on his chest. Kate rolled her suitcase behind him and they started their new adventure together.

After the truck was loaded with all of Kate's things, Duke gave her a moment to say goodbye. She stood in the empty room. Her white sneakers looked out of place in the now sea of brown that the room encompassed without any stuff in it.

Kate glanced at the closet where she had once spent hours trying to pick out what to wear on her very first date with Duke. She traced her hand along the windowsill and laughed at the memory of how she had been locked out. Kate walked to the door and with one palm on the door knob, she turned to gaze at the room.

"Thanks for the memories," she whispered half to herself and to the room.

Kate could barely look Zoe in the eye. They hugged and embraced one another. Sometimes, words just didn't cut it. The girls both held tears in their eyes and Zoe's boyfriend Joe laughed and rolled his eyes at them.

"You're going to live what, five minutes away from one another now?" he said.

They laughed.

"Yes, Joe. But that's not the point!" Zoe laughed. "I love you, OK?" she said to Kate.

"I know. I love you too."

Kate gave Joe a big bear hug and walked out of the front door. She reached for the sign on the front door as she went. It was the last item that she would take with her. A gift from her mom. A wooden plaque with the words *Beach House* inscribed in turquoise letters. Kate walked to the truck with the sign in hand and didn't look back as she said a whispered goodbye to her younger days.

Chapter 23
Home Sweet Home

Kate walked through the thick wooden door of her new home and dropped her bag and cell phone onto the end table nearby. She took a deep breath in and smelled the sweet musk scent that Duke's house always seemed to hold. She walked through the kitchen and out onto the back patio as Duke came in through the front door and started to unload a few of her boxes.

Kate breathed in the view that was around her. Birds chirped. The grass was green. Even the neighbours seemed like kind people as they bustled throughout the neighbourhood and drove their fancy cars up and down the streets. The faint smell of sea salt hung into the air. They weren't far from the ocean. *Some things never change*, she thought.

Kate had never experienced this much space in San Diego before. Her other two apartments were small and cramped. There had been no laundry. No privacy. This was different. Here she had more privacy than she knew what to do with. There were no bums on the street asking for money. There were no jewel-laden festival girls drunk from a late night-out. It was simply her. Her and Duke.

At that moment, Duke opened the sliding glass door and stepped onto the porch in his shiny black dress shoes. He smiled at Kate in her blue dress and matching earrings. As he stepped beside her and joined her on the back porch, Duke tugged one hand behind Kate's head and pulled her in to kiss him. Kate tilted her chin up to meet her new roommate's 6'4" frame and he cupped one hand at the small of her back.

Their kiss deepened. His hands slid lower. Kate sighed as she placed one hand around the area where his collar bone lay and slid a finger around his belt loop with the other as a tease. They looked at each other with a sparkle now in both of their eyes. Duke scooped Kate into his long arms with a steady ease. Her dark curls nestled into his chest as her arms wrapped around his neck and she felt as she had always wanted to. Small. Dainty. Like a princess.

Duke carried her easily up the stairs to their bedroom. He dropped Kate with a certain fervour onto the billowing bed and started to slide his hand underneath the skirt of her dress. They were good at this part of their relationship. Kate closed her eyes and felt the support of the soft white fabric that surrounded her entire body. She felt the hardness of Duke's warm body pressed up against hers. He had washboard abs, just like all of the boyfriends of the girls Kate had spent the last year serving coffee for.

Kate stared up at the tiled ceiling above her. They were alone at last. Kate's story had finally shifted. She had made it into the safe, loving arms of the man that she knew had always been waiting for her. She let a soft moan escape her lips in celebration of her new life.

Chapter 24
Hidden Agendas

It was now summer again. Time had passed quickly for Kate throughout the last few months. She opened the dresser that her and Duke shared and pulled out a pair of black yoga leggings and a colourful top. Her clothes were slightly wrinkled from the way the items had been shoved into the little rectangle container, crammed with too many pieces of clothing that she could not fit into the space.

Kate opened the top of the dresser and peeked into Duke's drawer. It was neat as a pin. As he was neat as a pin. Wool dress socks and silk boxer briefs were arranged in meticulous fashion. Kate lifted a stack of underwear and slid her hand underneath it as if checking to see if there was something else there besides clothing.

Kate couldn't quite shake the feeling that Duke had been hiding something from her lately. She had never snooped when she lived with Cal. Kate had always been confident that her relationship with him was all that he ever needed. She could feel this in the way that he looked at her after a long day of work, in the way he cooked dinner for her and the sweet way he tucked her curls behind her ear when she was falling asleep at night.

Duke was sweet with her, too. Although he was a very different man than Cal. Duke enjoyed the finer things in life. He was always working hard in order to provide the next best thing to create the image that he so desperately desired. She knew that Duke was attracted to her. Yet she would also catch him eying other women whenever they were out or watching the television. He didn't do it in a perverted way, but more because this was the way in which all men acted in this area of the city.

There had been a slight shift in their relationship after they moved in with one another. This was to be expected, Zoe had told Kate when she called her up one night when she was alone in the house. Kate spoke to Zoe on the phone from the closet as she looked around at the suits and dresses hanging around her. She wanted to make sure that Duke did not hear her speaking if he happened to walk through the door. Her closet had been a safe space for her as a child. She felt that now, in the same way, the small room seemed to enclose her into a cocoon of safety away from the rest of the world.

Duke was spending more time at the office now. He had just been offered a promotion at work and Kate was thrilled for him! At least, this was the feeling that she created when he was around her. Secretly, Kate could feel a growing coldness come between them and it scared her a bit.

Kate had earned a promotion at the yoga studio too after she had moved in with Duke. She was now working for the yoga studio manager, Jen, and she couldn't be more thrilled about it. Yoga gave Kate purpose. She felt at home at the studio and could tell that her students really enjoyed her classes.

It seemed that the trajectory of Kate's life was on the upswing. This was what she had always wanted, she told herself. Kate leaned her head against the back of the closet door. Duke would be home soon. She would make dinner for him. Something healthy (they were both watching their weight and had chosen to go vegan recently).

He would never know that she had rummaged through his things. She had been careful, as she always was. Yet, Kate wondered if he would even care if he found out? Kate pictured Cal's warm, brown hand and imagined it was caressing her back as she chopped spinach for the salad she was making.

Thirty minutes later, Duke walked through the front door with a bouquet of fresh flowers for Kate.

"Aww! Thank you so much. What a nice surprise." Kate smiled, kissed Duke on the cheek and rummaged through the cabinets for a vase. "How was your day?" Kate asked Duke.

"Good," Duke said. "Work was exhausting. Same old stuff." He grabbed a beer from the fridge and opened his laptop to check his email.

Duke didn't ask Kate how her day was. If he had, she would have told him about the older woman that took her yoga class and told her it had changed her life. But he did not ask. So instead, Kate grabbed a plate of food, caressed the back of Duke's head for a moment and walked into the living room to turn on the television.

Chapter 25
Career Success

The colder that Kate's home life got the more Kate's social life seemed to heat up. Her new position as an assistant to Jen came with an air of fame and fabulousness. Yoga was all the rage in San Diego. It seemed like every corner she turned on in this town, she saw a dozen guys and girls with rolled up yoga mats, scurrying their way to the nearest hot yoga class at the latest 'it' studio.

The popularity of the practice meant that Kate's new title gave her instant street credit in San Diego. Between teaching classes, organising supplies in the office and chatting with students at the front desk, she was now working close to sixty hours a week. At home, she was often on her phone answering questions from instructors or finishing up payroll. In her spare time, Kate would have coffee dates with different friends that she made from the yoga community.

Kate still made time to see Zoe. Their visits were more sporadic now. Yet every time that they saw each other, they still felt like no time had passed at all. Joe and Zoe were living blissfully. They fought every now and then, but they seemed to enjoy the passion that it created in their lives. Zoe's grandmother had gotten ill and so Zoe was spending more weekends in Los Angeles now helping out with her baby cousins.

"How are things with Duke?" Zoe asked Kate as the girls strolled through the local farmer's market and shopped through flowers and handmade soaps with coffees in hand.

"We're good," Kate said and she traced one finger around the top of her coffee cup. "We've both been super busy with work lately." Kate avoided telling Zoe about the unnerving coldness that she had increasingly sensed from Duke. She didn't have any proof. She was making it up in her head most likely, Kate thought to herself. So instead, Kate launched into a saga about work and a major yoga fiasco that she had averted last week in order to avoid the subject of her relationship.

Zoe had spent hundreds of hours observing Kate's facial expressions over the course of their friendship and she knew very well that something was wrong with Kate.

Some things are better left unsaid, she thought.

Zoe had noticed a shift in Kate since she had moved in with Duke. She was concerned for her friend. But in that moment, she simply grabbed Kate's hand and gave it an extra tight squeeze as they continued to talk about the yoga studio.

Chapter 26
Chasing Waterfalls

The next week, Kate was having a particularly rough week at work. She was incredibly busy. Her boss Jen was out of town and over the next seven days, it was Kate's responsibility to make sure the studio functioned to the best of her ability.

It did not help that Duke and Kate had gotten into a raging fight that morning. He had been spending nights out almost every week day over the past few weeks and it was getting on Kate's last nerve. Duke told her that he needed space. Kate knew that he thought she was needy. But she wasn't.

Kate was spending at least sixty hours a week at the yoga studio and several more of those hours with friends. She enjoyed her alone time. It was rather that she could feel her relationship with Duke crumbling the way that sand slipped through your fingertips at the beach. Quickly and without warning. The tighter you held on to the sand, the quicker it left from your palm. It was as if he were a ghost of the man she had once known. A man who had once desired her, once upon a time.

Kate was on her twelfth hour of work at the studio that day when she received a text from Duke. *"Heading out to dinner with Caitlin. Cool?"* It was, in fact, not cool. Duke knew it. This very matter had been what their raging fight had centred around that morning. Caitlin was a friend of Duke's from work. He had other female friends and yet something about his connection with her and the way that she acted gave Kate chills in a very creepy way.

Kate was burnt out from fighting and was focusing on filling a substitute teacher for the class that needed to be taught later that evening. She glanced at her phone and responded on autopilot. *"Sure…"* Kate knew the snarkiness and upset was obvious in her tone of voice even through text. Any normal boyfriend would have been able to see right through this age-old tactic. Duke responded back quickly, *"Cool. See you tonight."*

Kate slammed her phone onto her desk in the studio office. He was going to see her! This day could not get worse. She only had the energy to keep moving through her tasks until she could get into her car and drive home. As Kate gathered her things and started to walk down the stairs, she was stopped by her friend Sarah.

Sarah beamed at Kate and they chatted about upcoming events at the studio. Sarah was a magical human being. She was one of those people who had their head on straight. Yet somehow, the way that she was looking at Kate right now made her feel like she was one of those people. As if she had her life together just the same amount. As if she was someone that Sarah looked up to.

Kate gave a genuine smile back at her friend. "Call me tomorrow and I'll help you with your sequence. Anything I can do to help."

The girls exchanged a friendly farewell and as Kate reached the door of her CRV, she was hit with a gut-wrenching feeling. She knew. She knew at that very moment that her relationship was over. In the way that all women seem to have that sixth sense, she knew how the night with Caitlin would go for Duke. Perhaps, even worse, how all of the nights that he had been away from her had already gone.

This was new territory to navigate for Kate. She had never been cheated on before. All of her past boyfriends in New Mexico had been incredibly in love with her in a genuine way. Sure, they had their issues. But not this. This cold, aching, empty place that never seemed to quit.

On the drive home, Kate was feeling two extremely opposite feelings bubbling up inside of her. On one hand, she struggled to fight back tears as she felt the imaginary sucker punch to the gut she had just received. On the other hand, she felt a strange feeling of joy that seemed misplaced. It was related to the simple way that people noticed her now at the yoga studio. How she felt like she had a purpose. It was a place where people honoured and respected her and she could make a difference in their lives. Kate spent more time lately at the office than she did at home or with Duke. Then why did this sensation of abandonment hurt so painfully?

Kate walked up to the front door of her home as if she had seen a ghost. As if she may be a ghost herself. She wondered if this place had ever been her home at all. Perhaps, it was simply somewhere she had vacated for a small amount of her life. Like an Airbnb, or a summer camp dorm. A temporary moment in time. She was here for a moment just to learn some universal lesson in the experience of hell. Living with Duke had become the coldest place she had ever known.

An emotionally hollow Kate twisted the key into the lock and turned it as slowly as she could as if she were trying to delay the opening of a book that she did not want to read the ending to yet. Duke was nowhere to be found. It didn't matter. She knew. She sat on their couch and started to cry.

This cry was a lot different from the water faucet heart feeling that she had experienced before. This feeling was more primal. Guttural. Like a deer lying on the side of a road after it had been hit by a car. Like someone should come along and just put it out of its misery.

Kate cried like a new-born baby cries for a bottle of warm milk from its mother. Wild and unabashed. She was in incredible pain. She felt alone. She felt worse than alone. She felt held hostage in the home of a man who did not care about her any longer. Discarded, as if she were yesterday's recycling left to be taken out.

At least if she had lived alone, she would not feel this sick twisted sensation inside of her. Kate did not have the strength to dial Zoe's phone number. She simply sat like a statue on the couch and cried for hours and hours with no one to hear her but herself.

Around eleven p.m., Kate got a call from Duke. She hit the little green button to answer the call but she couldn't even form words. She simply cried into the receiver of the phone. Duke was irritated. He would be home in a moment, he said, with a cold and unconcerned tone. When Duke arrived, Kate continued to cry. She could not stop the tears. Duke went to bed. Kate continued to cry.

An hour later, as Duke lay fast asleep, Kate walked into the bathroom to blow her nose with more tissues. She looked into the mirror and could hardly recognise this girl staring back at her. She was empty. Hollow. Kate could barely make eye contact with this girl who seemed so sad, so hurt, so misused. Kate had been fun once. Adventurous. Sassy. What had happened to her? What had happened to that young girl that was once so very confident and sure of herself?

For a moment, Kate's thoughts took her to the alternate universe where she had chosen her life in a small town with Cal. Then Kate caught a glimmer out of the corner of her eye. Duke had left his cell phone charging in the corner of the bathroom. He never left his cell phone in here, Kate thought to herself. For a moment, she pondered whether or not Duke had done this on purpose. And suddenly the instinct of being a woman took over. She opened the phone and checked his text messages.

Kate's gag reflex activated as soon as she saw the little white bubble with the word 'Caitlin' sitting at the top of his messages. Below it, she noticed the messages from herself under the name 'Kate' with a little yellow wildflower sitting right next to it innocently. Her own messages were unread and even here, she saw the evidence she was looking for. That he had received the messages and had chosen not to respond.

Kate clicked open the messages from 'Caitlin'. She did a slow-motion lean over the bathroom countertop. The same countertop where Duke and Kate brushed their teeth together every evening. The shower behind her where they would luxuriously lather each other up with soap after long days of work. One hand of Kate's covered her own mouth as if to say to herself, "Please do not throw up."

The messages were bad. Even worse than Kate had expected. A woman's intuition is never wrong but she had certainly not planned for this. The messages between Caitlin and Duke went back over weeks. She could only imagine what had been deleted from the phone if this was what blatantly projected on the front of his screen.

Kate scrolled up to the messages from that very night. Her eyes landed on four numbers. 4432. An address. Caitlin's house. The message had come right after they had arrived at the restaurant together. The message was received at the same time that Kate had texted Duke and had never received a response. Kate threw up a little in her mouth.

She continued to scroll back through the incriminating evidence. Every red heart and flirty remark filled her with a burning rage that she had never really felt before. Kate was not a very angry person. The feeling was more primal than anything. Kate took the phone off of the charger and walked into the bedroom where Duke was peacefully sleeping in their bed.

"ASSHOLE!" Kate threw the phone at his head. She didn't even give Duke the chance to respond. She walked back into the bathroom, slammed the door shut, locked it and fell onto the rug beneath her.

The next morning, Kate awoke with imprints on her face from where she had fallen asleep on the bathroom rug. The tile was cold as she stood up and unlocked the door. Duke was already at work. Kate had to get to the studio as soon as possible for a full day of work. As she stood up, she was hit with a wave of nausea. She promptly turned to the sink and threw up over and over and over again until there was nothing left but yellow bile escaping from her lips.

Kate slid down the bathroom counter, frail and dehydrated. She couldn't move. The shock to her system had created an inability to move her body. It took all of the effort that Kate had within her to type up a text message to Sarah. *"Sick. Can't come in today. So sorry."*

Kate hit speed dial number one on her phone.

"WHAT. IS. WRONG?" Zoe's concerned voice came over the speaker phone. Her female intuition had kicked in right at the moment that she saw Kate's face pop up on her home screen and she knew that something terrible had happened.

"Please come here," Kate whimpered. She could barely get the words out.

Zoe knew what had happened. She had heard that same lifeless tone in a number of friends' voices after fateful moments such as this. "Don't worry. I will be there in fifteen. Don't go anywhere."

Fourteen minutes later, Zoe came to rescue Kate. They didn't waste any time pretending. Zoe walked into the bedroom that Kate shared with Duke and started to pack a duffel bag with her things. She wrapped Kate in a warm blanket that she had brought from their old home and ushered her out of the door, duffel bag in hand. They said nothing as Zoe drove away from the house and towards their old neighbourhood. She drove directly to their favourite drive-through and ordered two coffees and two veggie burritos to go.

At Zoe's home, they didn't need to talk about it. They could communicate everything that they needed to know about one another with one single glance. After a few hours sitting together, Kate could feel a little of her strength return to her. She opened Zoe's laptop and pulled open Craigslist. She scrolled for a moment, found the button for 'rentals' and clicked to open the tab.

Chapter 27
Mountains We Have Moved

Two days later, Kate returned to her home with Duke. He was gone at work. Zoe was gone, too. Kate stood in the house alone. She took a moment to collect her thoughts as she arrived in their bedroom. Kate took a deep inhale as she closed her eyes and slowly let it go. She pictured what a future with this man would have looked like. Nothing came to her mind. Instead, an image of a long dirt road in the country came to her mind and she saw herself in a pickup truck with Cal.

Kate walked to the bookshelf and touched a wooden sign. *"Everything is better when we are together!"* The sign seemed to be mocking Kate. Duke had given it to her a few months ago as a gift. She chortled viciously to herself as she started to open the dresser and remove her clothes from the inside. She filled her suitcase and a camping backpack with as many items as she could.

The plump bags rested against the door to the bedroom. There were still several items that she could not fit that remained in the house. Kate knew she was never coming back here. Yet, she did not have time or space to take all of the items. In one sick moment, Kate wanted to light a match and burn the house to the ground. In another, she thought about staying and begging Duke to fix things. Instead of making a decision either way, Kate walked over to the bookshelf, turned a loving hand toward the sign that Duke had given her, and placed it face down on the bookshelf. She promptly turned on her heel, grabbed her bags and waddled down the stairs under their weight and out the door. She slammed the door behind her without bothering to lock it and set her bags into the CRV.

Kate drove straight to the yoga studio with coffee in hand, and acted as though no events had transpired in the moments that she had been away. She pretended that she wasn't homeless and living out of her car. No one seemed to notice. In fact, no one seemed to be bothered at all. This thought comforted Kate as she slipped into the all-too-easy workaholic mode that she had grown accustomed to incorporating into her everyday life.

The next morning, Kate drove into a hippie neighbourhood in the city and parked outside of the apartment listing that she had found online. The ocean gleamed further down the road and palm trees swayed in the breeze like a peaceful oasis. Kate stepped up to the apartment door with a check book in her hand. She had now lived in San Diego long enough to know exactly how these kinds of interactions were to be proceeded.

The apartment was everything Kate had dreamt of and everything that was advertised online. Kate felt that she must have a guardian angel looking out for her. This listing was the first that she had seen.

Kate greeted the real estate agent warmly who told her to take a look around. The upper-level apartment was bathed in golden, healing light from the sunshine that streamed in through the windows. Kate's heels clacked against the wooden floorboards in a pleasurable way and the ocean waves nearby could be heard through the open window in the bedroom.

A young couple walked in after Kate to view the listing. A moment of fear lurched into Kate's gut as she realised that she was not the only one seeking out this apartment. The couple took one look around at the small living room and looked to the real estate agent.

"Too small." The couple promptly walked out of the front door and down the steps.

"I'll take it!" Kate beamed. "It's perfect." She pulled out her check book and signed for the rent in full.

One week later, Kate was fully moved into her new apartment. She didn't have much furniture, but it was perfect to her all the same. Kate had never lived in a space that was truly hers before. She had inevitably spent a large chunk of time alone in her first apartment in San Diego, but that was not by choice. She had been too stricken with grief after losing Cal to enjoy the space at all. Here, she felt differently.

In her new apartment, there was no one to tell Kate when to do the dishes or how to mop the floor. She did not need to feel embarrassed by the way her hair frizzed in the morning or the black makeup lines that always smudged underneath her eyes after a night of sleep. She could play whatever music she wanted. Her closet was filled with beautiful fabrics and she could choose to wear any of the items wherever she wanted to go. If she wanted to stay in, well, she could do that too.

Kate flopped onto her bed and opened up social media. She snapped a photo of herself in bed with white linen flowing all around her. A single word made up her caption as she hit the button to post the photo. *"Home."*

Chapter 28
Happily Ever After

The next morning, Kate rolled over and hit the snooze button on her alarm clock. 7.25 a.m. She sat up and stretched her arms over her head. Sunlight streamed in through the windows of her second-storey beach apartment. She jumped out of her bed, patted down the fluffy white comforter and smiled as she opened the window.

The sound of ocean waves rolled lazily into her bedroom. The palm trees swayed in the balmy California breeze. The Pacific Ocean sparkled back at her and this time, she knew it was whispering to her, "You belong here."

Kate clicked the coffee pot on to brew and started to pick out her outfit for the day. She squirmed into black yoga leggings and a rose-coloured top. As Kate held the turquoise gemstone against her neck with one hand, she used the other to check her work email. She quickly responded to a message from her boss Jen as she wrapped a blue sweatshirt around her arms.

Kate poured herself a mug of coffee to go. She grabbed two apples and a protein bar and shoved them into her bag. There were a few dishes in her sink to wash when she got home but nothing major. Kate slung her bag around her shoulder, tucked a curl behind her right ear and smiled to herself as she walked out of her front door and down the steps.

Kate checked the lock a few times as she turned the key to the left. She would not return until later that evening. She waved to Jet, her surfer-bum, next-door neighbour, and he seemed happy just to be alive. "Another beautiful day!" He laughed at her and Kate giggled right back to him.

Kate loaded her things into her blue CRV and set her coffee mug carefully into the centre console to make sure it was secure before she started. As she got behind the wheel, she navigated to a dead-end road with a small stretch of rocky ocean before her. Kate put the CRV in park, turned off the ignition and pulled the emergency break up.

The twenty-two-year-old girl took a deep breath and sighed. Her eyelashes fluttered tightly against her cheeks and tears began to fall softly into her lap. She opened her door for a moment to smell the slight salt in the air that always existed in Southern California. She grabbed her mug of coffee and took a slow, steady sip.

Kate wondered if this was what it was supposed to feel like. To be truly in love. In love with this life that was fully hers. Her dreams. Her fumbles. Her grief. It would have been so much easier to give up. To have chosen the life in New Mexico that was written for her.

She thought of Cal for a moment and missed his sweet voice. Even now, she knew that if he were in the seat next to her, he would be cheering her on in the most uplifting way.

"You did it, babe! I knew that you could."

She imagined that he was saying exactly those words to her in some far-off land at that very moment. Perhaps, in another universe, they were doing just that.

But Kate was here now. In this place. This beautiful place. All alone. She thought back to all of the painful moments that had happened to her throughout the last year. She felt her cheeks flush and embarrassment rush over her as she thought about her first time driving on the interstate in California and the cars that honked around her.

It occurred to Kate that she very easily could have never experienced this moment at all. It would have been so much easier to stay in New Mexico. Life would have been easier. Simplistic. Quintessential.

As Kate went to turn on the car again, she realised that she had never been more alone than she was at this very moment in time. Kate's eyes darted to a single yellow wildflower hanging off the seaside cliff in front of her. The CRV backed up and Kate heard a buzzing sound come from her phone. This most certainly meant that Jen had just texted her about the plans for the day.

Kate took one last gaze into her rear-view mirror and paused before she drove away. Her eyes met the very place where the horizon met the ocean. Her heart welled up for a moment.

"Thank you," she whispered softly to the sparkling blue water, "I'm so happy that I'm here."